Missing Legacy

Steampunk OZ: Book 6

by Steve DeWinter

I0625910

Summary

In this action-packed second season of Steampunk OZ, American author S.D. Stuart returns to the Australis Penal Colony, where an ancient, and devastating, weapon was hidden a millennium ago.

Book 6

Unable to even begin his quest, Caleb is ready to abandon his birthright to the throne when a new enemy emerges.

This book is a work of fiction. References to real people, events, establishments, organization, or locales are intended only to provide a sense of authenticity, and are used fictitiously. All other characters, and all incidents and dialogue, are drawn from the author's imagination and are not to be construed as real.

eBook Edition

ISBN-10: 1-61978-042-9

ISBN-13: 978-1-61978-042-2

Paperback Edition

ISBN-10: 1-61978-043-7

ISBN-13: 978-1-61978-043-9

Chapter 1

Caleb looked out the window of the airship as it descended. As promised, the Southern Marshal said he was free to leave the colony, but that also meant he had to leave the Southern Territories.

And he had to do it without Dorothy.

He was returning to the hybrid colony one last time to gather his belongings before the Southern Marshal's airship took him over the wall and back into the rest of OZ.

He didn't plan to stay out of the Southern Territories for very long. Just long enough to gather an army and return for Dorothy.

He didn't recognize the town rising up to meet the airship and quickly calculated they were landing too soon.

He made his way forward to the cockpit.

"Your instructions were to take me directly to the colony."

The pilot didn't turn around but kept his attention locked on the window of the cockpit. "I'm not taking this ship anywhere near that much smoke."

Caleb followed the pilot's gaze and his heart thumped heavily in his chest. Thick columns of black smoke rose along the horizon, as if half the hybrid colony had been set ablaze.

The pilot continued. "There will be a carriage when we land that will take you the rest of the way."

"And how long will that be?"

"Longer if you don't leave the cockpit and let me do my job."

Caleb absentmindedly chewed on the piece of fingernail he'd bitten off while waiting for the airship to land. He bounded down the ramp before it touched the ground and searched for the carriage that should be waiting for him.

There were no horses. There was no carriage.

He approached the group of men tethering down the airship. He singled out the man who was directing the other men as they struggled to keep the airship steady while others tied the tether ropes to a large truck. Once the airship was tied down to the tether truck, one man could drive the truck to reposition the airship anywhere they needed.

He tapped the foreman's shoulder.

"There's supposed to be a carriage waiting here."

The foreman looked him over with a frown. "What do you want me to do about it?"

"Where is it?"

The foreman glanced at him. "We're a little busy right now?"

Caleb grabbed the foreman's shoulder.

"I must have that carriage immediately."

The foreman knocked Caleb's hand away with his arm and took a step back. "Do we have a problem?"

Caleb held his hands up, palms out. "No. No problem. I'm sorry."

"Good. You just be glad we got here in time to tether the ship. Anything else can wait."

Chuffing sounds drew Caleb's attention to the tether truck that blew white puffs of steam from the boiler while it idled in position as the men tied the airship tethers to it. He remembered watching an airship launch from a tether truck before. The tether hooks on the truck were spring-loaded and controlled by mechanism in the driver's cabin that allowed all the tether lines for an airship to be released simultaneously. While it took an entire ground crew for an airship to land, mechanizing the launch process meant that, once an airship was tethered to the truck, one man could tow the airship to the launching field and release it from the controls inside.

Caleb glanced up and down the road. He could see a kilometer in both directions.

Neither way showed that a carriage was on its way here.

The hybrid colony was burning and he was too far away to help.

A metal clanging sound drew his attention back to the tether truck as someone loaded more logs into the firebox, which heated the boiler, before slamming the iron door shut again and joining the rest of the crew in tethering the last of the ropes to the truck.

Caleb studied the group of men. Those who had finished tying ropes to the truck had gathered around the foreman, the same man who had shooed him away earlier. Nobody was paying attention to him. Nor were they paying attention to the fact that he was slowly making his way to the front of the tether truck.

Caleb considered himself to be smarter than most, and he'd seen men with more brawns than brains operate a tether truck. How hard could it be?

He took one last look around to confirm that nobody was paying attention to him and hopped into the cabin of the steam-powered tether truck. He grasped the steering wheel with both hands and scanned his eyes over the numerous gauges in the dashboard before him. Each gauge had a needle that twitched to show the status of things he knew nothing about.

He quickly realized he had no idea how to make the carriage move. He twisted the steering wheel back and forth like he'd seen drivers do anytime a horseless carriage went by on the street.

Nothing happened. The truck stayed perfectly still.

He could feel his heart pounding heavily in his chest. He frantically searched for any indication of what made the truck move. He could see only two levers. One stuck up out of the floor by his seat and the other protruded from the dash.

He glanced out the dirt-smeared window and saw that the last of the tether lines had been secured to the truck. All of the men huddled together, except for the foreman, who broke from the group and headed for the truck. If the foreman caught him trying to steal the truck, he would definitely decide that they had a problem.

Caleb reached out and yanked on the lever on the dash. Several angry shouts came from the group of men who scrambled to grab the tether lines he had just released before the airship floated away without a pilot on board.

A quick glance over his shoulder confirmed the foreman was now running toward the truck yelling at him to get out.

Caleb grabbed the second lever and shoved it forward. The pilot of the airship had chosen to land at the top of a low hill, so when Caleb released the brake, the truck began to roll forward down the hill.

Behind him, several men joined the foreman in running after the truck and barking orders at him to stop.

Even if he knew how to stop the truck's accelerating descent down the hill, he would have refused. The colony needed him now, more than ever, and he was going to do everything he could to get there before it was too late.

Of course, he would need to learn how to stop this thing sooner or later. Preferably, sooner.

As the truck barreled downhill at increasing speed, he twisted the wheel back and forth and felt the truck lurch from side to side. He quickly discovered that small adjustments of the wheel kept him going, more or less, in a straight path down the hill.

He looked back with relief to see he was leaving the men far behind. But he was almost out of hill and the ground was leveling out. The truck was starting to slow down and he still had no idea how to make it move under its own power.

He frantically searched around inside the cabin of the truck, but he'd already pulled the only two levers he could see. The truck slowed to a fast walking speed, and was still slowing down.

He jumped forward in his seat, trying to force the truck forward with his own body weight. It was no use. The ground had leveled out and all the momentum gained from the hill had been spent. The truck rolled to a dead stop.

He craned his neck back to see the men still running down the hill after him. If he couldn't get this thing moving again, they would catch up with their stolen truck and most likely take their frustration out on him. As he twisted back around in his seat, his foot hit something on the floor and the truck lurched forward a couple of feet before stopping again.

He peeked under the steering wheel and saw there were two more levers poking up out of the floorboard. He tentatively pushed down on the first lever with his foot and nothing happened. He pushed it all the way down to the floor and still nothing happened. Leave it up to the humans to create something with extra levers that didn't do anything.

He pushed down on the other lever with a little more confidence and the truck shot forward, throwing him back into his seat and knocking his foot off the pedal. The truck motored down to a stop again.

A quick glance behind saw the fastest of the men were already at the bottom of the hill. But all was not lost. He knew how to make the truck go.

He eased his foot down on the lever, and the truck rolled forward under its own power. It didn't take long for him to learn how to alternate pushing on the pedal and easing up on it to keep the truck going at a more controlled speed.

Stopping was another matter, but one he didn't need to worry about until he got to his destination.

Caleb motored along through the countryside, and as he got closer to the colony, what he had feared before was becoming the reality. The amount of smoke billowing up from inside the boundary of the electrified fence could mean only one thing. Half the colony was already in flames.

He pushed the lever all the way to the floor and clung to the steering wheel as he fought to keep the truck on the dirt road that led to the hybrid colony.

A mad buzzing sound erupted from inside the dashboard right before there was a loud pop and several of the needles spun wildly in the gauges. The truck lurched under him followed by the loud hiss of steam escaping the boiler. He pushed down several times on the lever that made the truck go, but this time nothing happened.

The truck rolled to a stop in the middle of the road and nothing he did made any difference.

He was close enough to smell the fires burning inside the colony. And if he was close enough to smell it, he was close enough to run the rest of the way on foot.

He crested the low hill and caught sight of the main gate to the colony. Hybrids were walking out of the burning compound; single file.

It didn't look like everyone was carrying everything they owned, but it certainly looked like everything they carried was now all they owned.

He ran down the line toward the front gate. Nobody talked as they walked. Even the children labored under their belongings as they shuffled alongside their parents. Anyone who made eye contact with him as he ran, rather than say hello like they usually did, quickly looked away.

Even though the only houses that burned were on the far side of the colony, he could feel the heat from the fires that hungrily consumed the hybrid village. And it chilled him to his bones.

Up ahead, Zee guided the small horse that pulled a hay wagon filled with her family's possessions.

She spotted him running toward her and ducked her head as she urged the horse to move faster.

"Zee, what's going on?"

She ignored him and pulled harder on the heavy noseband of the horse's hackamore, a bit-less bridle. The horse responded by bucking his head and stamping a front foot.

Caleb grabbed Zee by the shoulders. "Talk to me Zee."

She twisted out of his grip. "I have nothing to say to you."

He stepped in front of her, blocking her. "What happened?"

Her eyes pierced his, water forming around the edges as tears welled up. "You want to know what happened?"

Her sudden ferocity took him by surprise. He nodded his head slightly, unsure if he really wanted the answer or not.

"I'll tell you what happened. You happened!"

"Zee, I…"

She shoved him back violently. "Shut up! Just shut up! You don't get to talk, you get to listen. Are you going to listen? Or am I wasting my time?"

He relaxed his balled fists and tried to look as nonthreatening as possible as he nodded silently.

"You want to know what's happening here? I'll tell you. We are running and hiding, erasing any trace that we were here, because our chosen leader refuses to lead us."

He opened his mouth and she put up a hand. "You don't get to speak. You haven't earned that right."

He closed his mouth and let her continue.

"A secret cabal of world leaders, known only as the Directors, are coming. They want the Brahmastra. And once they have it, they will use it to kill all of us before conquering the rest of the world."

The words escaped his lips before he could stop them. "Why kill us?"

She ignored his infraction. "We are hiding from them because we are the only ones who still know how to use it. We needed you to get it before they did."

Allowing him to speak a moment before emboldened him to try again. "But why me?"

"There is a girl whose blood is needed to unlock the box that contains the Brahmastra. You were supposed to take her with you and get it before the Directors could steal it from us again."

"But why me? Why am I the only one who could do this among all the hybrids?"

"It had to be you, because the girl asked for you by name. She said she would only help us if you went along to help her."

He shook his head, clearly not getting the point she was trying to make.

"Why would she ask for me? I don't even know who this girl is."

She exhaled sharply in exasperation. "Yes you do. It's Dorothy."

Chapter 2

Deep in the bowels of the Southern Marshal's castle, Caleb urged the guard in front of him to walk faster as they made their way through the maze of underground passageways. As soon as they reached the door to Nero's underground warehouse, Caleb brushed past the guard and took the steps two at a time down into the partially lit chamber.

His feline eyes adjusted quickly to the dim light, yet the true depth of the warehouse remained unknown. He had never managed to reach the other end of the warehouse the last time he was down here. The multitude of odd trinkets, contraptions and carvings, from civilizations long since dead, could have stretched on into infinity for all he knew.

Nero remained seated on a stool with his back to the door. He was at the table that held the large stack of ancient scrolls and sat bent over an open scroll, a magnifying optical lens clutched in his scarred hand. Caleb wasn't sure he had even heard him come in until his raspy voice broke the silence. "What changed your mind?"

"You could've told me Dorothy was going on your little escapade."

Nero kept his back to Caleb and continued to study his scroll. "Would that have made a difference?"

"If I knew you were going to put her life in danger, I would have…"

Caleb let his words fade to silence. He would what? He was a prisoner in the

Southern Territories, despite the best efforts of everyone to convince him otherwise.

Nero finally stopped studying his scroll and faced him. He parroted the same thing that was running through Caleb's head.

"And just what would you have done?"

This line of thinking was going to get him nowhere. If he wanted to keep Dorothy safe, he had to come up with something else.

Nero placed the magnifying glass on the table and stood up with considerable effort.

"Her father built the box that contains the Brahmastra. Her blood is the key to opening that box."

"I won't let you kill her."

"Who said anything about killing her? We only need a few drops of her blood. She will barely miss it."

"Why don't you bring the box to her? Why does she have to go anywhere?"

"The box her father built is big and heavy. The Brahmastra is much smaller than that. Much smaller. Believe me when I tell you, getting her to the box will be far simpler than bringing the box to her."

"Okay, so we get this Brahmastra first and stop the bad guys. Then what?"

"That subject has been a matter of debate for the past couple of days. The Southern Marshal wants to keep it to ensure the protection of the hybrids. I, however, disagree. As long as the Brahmastra is accessible, it can be stolen."

"Then we destroy it."

Nero shook his head. "It cannot be destroyed. I say, after we have stopped the Directors, we drop it in the deepest hole and, this time, don't spread stories and legends about what it does and where to find it."

This was a side of Nero he had never seen before. It surprised him that Nero was not even considering keeping this weapon for himself. It was like the old Nero had burned away along with his skin and from the ashes was born a new man.

He'd spent his whole life trusting a man who didn't deserve to be trusted. Now, he found it hard to trust the same man who had undergone a dramatic transformation and was finally proving to be trustworthy. Or was he just putting on an act?

"We could always keep it and claim to drop it down a deep hole."

Nero shook his head like a father who had just been asked by his child if they could have chocolate cake for breakfast.

"It is too powerful a weapon for anyone to possess. The Directors sent me here to find it. Why do you think I took so long? I didn't want them to have it."

Maybe it was possible that Nero had changed.

"So you don't plan to keep it?"

"After we have stopped the Director's invasion, we will try to destroy it. If that doesn't work, we will put it where no one will ever find it again."

"And just where could that be?"

"There are active volcanoes four thousand kilometers southwest of OZ. We take an airship, sail right over one of them, and drop it in. It won't be destroyed, but at least it will be inaccessible."

Caleb had to admit to himself, Nero had given this a lot of thought. If he truly wanted to keep this weapon out of everyone's hands, including his own, then Caleb would help him. But there was still one thing he needed to secure.

"What about Dorothy?"

"What about her?"

"Once you have the Brahmastra, will Dorothy be free?"

"Once she has opened the box her father created, her job is done. All that I ask is that you bring the Brahmastra to me before the two of you disappear."

It sounded like a good plan, even though he knew nothing of the details. But if all he had to do was get this ancient artifact and bring it back to Nero to free Dorothy, the details didn't really matter.

Nero clapped a hand on his back. "I see it in your eyes you have already decided to help. Splendid. Come with me and I'll introduce you to the rest of your team."

"The rest?"

The skin around Nero's mouth stretched as he attempted to smile. "You didn't think I was going to send you out there all alone, did you?"

Nero plucked a torch off the wall and headed into the darkness of the infinite warehouse. Caleb caught up with him.

"Are we going to the other end of the warehouse?"

Nero took a few more steps in silence and then paused at an empty torch holder on the wall.

"Not quite."

He placed the torch in the holder, and using the torch for leverage, twisted the holder thirty degrees to the left. Caleb watched the stone wall in anticipation, half expecting it to slide inward or split open to reveal a secret passageway.

The ground rumbled under his feet as the wall slid up. But it wasn't just the wall that slid up; the entire warehouse seemed to be rising. He quickly realized that the warehouse wasn't rising. Instead, the section of floor where he and Nero stood was dropping.

They continued down for twenty feet before the wall around the circular stone platform ended at the ceiling of another underground chamber.

Electric lamps sparked to life and illuminated a large glass and brass cylinder lying on its side. The cylinder rested in an indentation in the floor with one end pointed at a tunnel opening cut into the wall.

Nero hobbled over to the glass cylinder and grabbed the brass handle that stuck out on the side. He slid part of it sideways to reveal red velvet seats that looked like they belonged in a carriage. In fact, the inside of the cylinder looked exactly like the inside of a carriage. But this carriage had neither wheels nor room for any horses on either end.

The inside looked more like a carriage than the outside. It had the standard two bench seats that faced each other, but, unlike a carriage, there was a small instrument panel in between the two seats with a single red button.

Nero looked at him expectantly. "If you've never traveled by tube, you've never traveled in style."

Caleb stepped into the cylinder and started to sit down. Nero motioned to the seats on the other side of the compartment.

"You always want to face in the direction of travel. Trust me."

Caleb sat down in the rear seat of the carriage. Nero slid the curved door closed, sat down next to him, and looked at him with a playful expression in his eyes.

"When was the last time you ate?"

That was a weird question. Rather than wait for him to respond, Nero pushed the single red button while Caleb answered without giving it much thought.

"About four hours, why?"

Nero faced forward and leaned his head against the back of the seat as he closed his eyes. "Good. Velvet is really hard to clean."

Caleb's ears popped from the sudden change of air pressure. Through the glass that enclosed the cylinder, he could see dust being sucked into the tunnel opening. The cylinder rumbled forward slowly until the leading-edge hit the edge of the tunnel.

Only past experience could've prepared him for what happened next. Unfortunately, this was his first time. His head slammed against the back of his seat as the cylinder shot forward through the tunnel. He realized why Nero had closed his eyes. There was no source of illumination anywhere inside or outside the cylinder and it was completely dark. There was nothing to see anyway.

Even with nothing to tell him which way was up, he still felt as if they had gone upside down a few times as the cylinder rocketed through the pitch black underground tunnel. Only the momentum that kept him pinned to his seat prevented him from being thrown around the inside of the cylinder as the tunnel curved and twisted.

His ears popped again and he felt gravity regain control as the cylinder slowed. Through the glass ahead, he saw a faint circle of light grow larger as they got closer until it engulfed the cylinder and they jerked to a stop in the brightly lit chamber.

While Caleb waited for his eyes to adjust to the sudden brightness, Nero unlatched the cylinder door and slid it open.

"Welcome to my underground lair. Be sure to hold on to the handrails."

Caleb blinked a few times and everything came into focus. He stepped out of the cylinder carriage and into a massive laboratory.

There was the faint hum of electricity all around him. One entire wall was covered with tall metal boxes, each replete with a mishmash of gauges and dials. Spaced several feet apart along the outer walls were tall metal spires that encircled the entire laboratory. Arcs of electricity shot from one tall metal spire to another. The unnaturally made lightning bolts didn't just spark from one spire to the next, occasionally one would arc diagonally across the laboratory to a spire on the opposite wall.

Nero was completely unfazed by any of this as he made his way through the room. He gripped the brass handrail that ran the whole length from the carriage platform to a small door on the other side of the room. Nero tripped unsteadily over some loose cables on the floor. The only thing keeping him from falling flat on his face was the handrail he clung to with all his might.

He paused at the center of the room and looked back. "Come, you have to meet the rest of your team."

Chapter 3

Nero disappeared through the door on the other side of the laboratory, completely unharmed by the artificial lightning crackling all around him. Caleb had even seen several small lightning bolts emanate from Nero and connect with the top of the closest spire. But Nero had continued through the room as if none of it had happened.

Maybe the room looked scarier than it really was. Maybe all the electricity arcing across the room was as harmless as the glow from a faint light bulb.

Caleb let go of the brass handle on the cylinder carriage and the fur over his entire body immediately stuck straight out right before a blast of lightning hit him square in the chest, knocking him back into the carriage.

So much for the harmless theory.

He scrambled to his feet quickly inside the carriage and tasted the sweet rusty flavor of blood from where he had bit his tongue. He smelled something burning, looked down at himself, and quickly patted out the smoldering bits of fur where the lightning had impacted him.

He looked out the carriage door at the bolts of lightning that sparked gleefully like specters all around the laboratory. It was only then that he noticed the numerous warning signs mounted in every conceivable place claiming "High-Voltage", "Danger", and "Risk of Electrocution."

He leaned closer to the door and his fur lifted as it was drawn toward the electricity that ricocheted from one wall to another across the room. He placed his hand on the brass handle of the door and his fur settled back down.

So that's how Nero had managed to get through the room without a problem. He had no fur. His burnt and scarred flesh must have created some form of insulating layer that protected him from the electricity that crackled through every crevice of this room. Caleb's body was covered in nothing but fur. He needed something to wrap around himself that would insulate him from the electricity if he was going to make it through this room too.

He searched the carriage, but everything was mounted to something else in there. There was nothing loose he could grab to fend off the lightning.

He held onto the brass handle so he could get closer to the door without drawing a fiery spark of hot electric death to him. His eyes searched the platform just outside the cylinder carriage for something, anything that would protect him from the lightning.

He spotted a wool blanket on the edge of a desk about twenty feet from the carriage doorway. Wool was an excellent insulator, which meant it was a horrible conductor. Maybe if he wrapped that blanket around his entire body, he could make it through the room without his fur attracting any lightning.

But he had to get to the blanket first. And he couldn't do that if he got zapped as soon as he took his hand off the carriage's brass door handle.

With his hand on the handle, he stared into the electrified room and watched the lightning dance. As he watched, he noticed a cyclical pattern to the electricity. Most of it seemed to concentrate together as it traveled the room. He watched the largest concentration of electrical energy make its way around the room like the sweeping hand of a clock. Was this an optical illusion, or was there a potential lull in electrical activity at short periodic intervals? Would this allow enough time for him to get to the blanket and isolate himself from the electrical current that crackled throughout the air?

He focused on the highest concentration of energy and, when it was on the opposite end of the room, he lifted his hand away from the brass door handle. He silently counted to ten before his fur started to rise. He grabbed the brass handle and his fur lay down immediately. When the focal point of electricity was directly above the cylinder carriage platform, he let go of the handle. His fur stuck out immediately and small sparks shot between the extended individual hairs right before he grabbed the handle again.

There was a cyclical pattern to the electricity in the room. One that he could take full advantage of.

Maybe this was a test? Maybe figuring out the pattern of energy in the room, and using it to get to the blanket so he could pass safely through the room, was all a test to prove he was the one.

If it took being the one to help Dorothy, then he would be the one. He would prove himself worthy.

He watched the electricity circle the room a few more times, trying to gauge how long he could risk being away from the carriage before he was in danger. He let a few more opportunities pass as he counted silently while he envisioned himself running to grab the blanket and returning to the carriage. No matter how quickly he imagined himself running for the blanket, none of the scenarios in his head allowed any time for the return trip to the carriage. What he was planning to do could only be considered successful as a one-way trip.

He only had enough time to reach the blanket, and wrap it around his body, before the highest concentration of electricity reached him.

There was very little room for error, including the potentially mistaken concept that the blanket might insulate him from the electricity that coursed angrily throughout the room.

He had one chance to make the right decision, or risk being fried to a crisp. There would be no second chances.

Nero had already crossed the room unharmed, proving it could be done. But then again, he didn't have fur covering his entire body that made him a magnet for the deadly lightning bolts.

His heart pounded in his throat as he crouched, readying himself to make a mad dash for the wool blanket.

All his focus was on the concentration of electricity. As soon as it was at the farthest point from him in the room, Caleb made his move.

He shot out of the carriage like a bullet and ran full speed for the blanket. His whole body tickled as he felt his fur rise up.

He raced to the blanket and yanked it off the table. Or at least he tried to. His shoulder strained as the blanket came partially off the table before it resisted and pulled back. But it hadn't pulled back. It just would not come fully off the table.

He stared in disbelief at the nails that fastened the blanket to the table. The first sign that he was in more trouble than he could handle was the sickly sweet smell of the air ionizing around him.

He slammed his eyes shut as hard as he could, but the blinding flash still left an afterimage on his retinas right before the snaking whip of lightning threw him across the room.

He didn't have a chance to regain his footing before another blasts sent him sprawling across the floor. His goose was, literally, being cooked. He could smell his fur burning as one bolt of lightning after another slammed into him in rapid succession.

There were times, when the body was subjected to horrors beyond imagination, the brain took a vacation and separated itself from what was happening to the body. This was what Caleb was experiencing right now. As his impending death weighed down heavily on his soul, he thought only of Dorothy and how he had let her down.

His body slammed into something hard right before his head came to rest on something soft. Strangely enough, there were no more bolts of lightning tossing him around like a rag doll. But, despite the nonstop pounding, he hadn't been killed.

He opened his eyes and found himself staring at the red velvet seat inside the carriage. He tenderly lifted his head and inspected himself. His fur was singed in several places, but the burns were not severe. Instead of killing him, the multitude of lightning strikes had pushed him back into the carriage. The defenses of this room were not designed to kill anyone, only to keep them out.

But keep them out of what? He looked out of the carriage at the door on the other side of the electrified room. That was the same door Nero had easily gone through not five minutes before.

So this room was some kind of test. And since he wasn't dead, it looked like Caleb was being given a second chance. A second chance that he wouldn't squander like he had the first. He had to prove that he was worthy of the quest that Nero was going to send him on. He had to prove he had the strength, and the intelligence, to achieve the goal.

As had already been shown to him on his first attempt, he couldn't conquer this room with strength alone. He had to use his smarts. This time he studied the room, looking for something he'd missed before.

How had Nero managed to get through this room unscathed? What had he done differently as he made his way to the other side?

And then he remembered what Nero had said right before leaving the carriage. He looked into the laboratory and saw the brass hand rail Nero clung to when he had moved through the room. Originally, Caleb had dismissed this simple action as the needs of an old man who had trouble walking and seemed to cling to everything around him as he moved about. This time, Nero had not clung to the brass railing only because of the damage to his body. It must've somehow protected him from the lightning. That railing must have grounded him and made him invisible to the electricity that crackled in the air.

Caleb cautiously reached a hand out to the railing that stretched all the way from the door on the other side of the room to the door of the carriage. The fur on his arm stood up as he reached out of the carriage. As soon as he touched the brass rail, his hair settled back down and he was not pummeled with bolts of electricity.

Keeping a hand firmly on the rail, he walked across the room and made it all the way to the door on the far side without incident.

The door opened just as he arrived and Nero stood in the threshold. "You took long enough."

Caleb grimaced. "Was this a test?"

"Not really. I told you what to do as we are getting out of the carriage." Nero disappeared through the door and Caleb hurried to follow him, glad to leave the lightning room behind.

The hallway beyond the door was short and opened quickly into a brightly lit room filled with plush chairs and a sofa along one wall.

Seated on the sofa, and looking expectantly at him, was Dorothy.

Chapter 4

The room Nero had led him to was completely white. White walls, white floor, white ceiling. Even the few overstuffed chairs and the one sofa along the far wall were white. No tables, no pictures, nothing. It was the strangest sensation to be in a room devoid of color. It made him feel strange to be dressed in the black and brown leather outfit that was common in the hybrid colony. Animals in the wild lived or died on whether they could blend in to their environment, but this new environment was one in which he could not hide. He had never felt more out of place.

Dorothy, dressed all in white herself, slowly stood up from the sofa. Caleb closed his eyes, fully expecting her to disappear when he reopened them. He opened them slowly and let out the breath he had been holding when he saw she was still there.

"Hello Caleb."

He rushed over to her and they wrapped their arms around each other. He inhaled her scent and the months they had spent apart evaporated.

Nero hobbled across the room and paused at the opening to a side hallway. "I will leave you two alone… to discuss things."

Caleb barely registered Nero had left as he hugged Dorothy. He'd spent months trying to find her and now, when they were finally together, he didn't know what to say. But it didn't matter. Words weren't needed.

A bark echoed from the same hallway Nero had gone down. They both looked toward the sound, the clatter of claws scraping against polished floor tiles echoed off the walls. Whatever was coming down that hallway was running straight for them. Caleb released her and widened his stance, ready for anything to emerge from the hallway.

A large dog, big enough that it could have been a wolf, bounded into the room. It skidded to a stop on the smooth tile floor and locked eyes with Caleb. The dog's black fur, speckled with gray, rose up on his back as he growled. Caleb let out an involuntary hiss.

Dorothy's voice broke the tension in the room. "Who's a good boy?"

The dog's head whipped around and his tail began wagging ferociously as his paws slid on the smooth tiles while trying to run faster than the polished floor would allow. He leaped the remaining couple of feet through the air and tackled Dorothy back down to the couch, licking her face and making her laugh.

"Who's a good boy? That's right. Toto's a good boy."

Caleb resisted the urge to vomit as Toto… A dog!… slobbered all over her.

She continued to muss up the fur on Toto's head while blowing in his face, causing him to lick her even more.

It was disgusting.

Caleb cleared his throat loudly.

She stopped fawning over Toto and they both looked over at Caleb. Toto emitted a deep growl.

Dorothy patted him on the back. "Easy there, boy."

Emboldened by the approval of his master, Toto barked at Caleb.

Dorothy barked her command just as loudly. "Toto, sit!"

Toto flopped to the floor in utter compliance. Caleb's keen sense of hearing detected the subsonic growl just under the dog's breath.

Dorothy leaned back on the couch and lounged comfortably. "So, you've agreed to help?"

Caleb tore his eyes from Toto and looked at Dorothy. "I haven't agreed to anything. In fact, I'm here to talk you out of it."

She sat forward again. "You can't talk me out of it. I made a deal with the Southern Marshal. If I do this, we get our freedom."

"We can find another way. Now that we're together…"

"I asked for you because I needed someone I could trust. Someone who would be there for me, no matter what happened."

"You don't have to do this."

"Did Nero tell you what was at stake?"

"Of course he did. But there has to be another way. We can bring the box to you…"

"There's not enough time for that. Nero explained everything and I agree with him. The only way to get this artifact before these Directors is for me to open the box where it is. The artifact inside is much smaller, and we can travel quicker without a heavy box."

"I still don't get why you have to be the one to open the box?"

"When my father built that box, he encoded it so that only our blood can trigger the lock. But he is too weak to travel."

Caleb was about to reply when his brain shifted gears as to what Dorothy had just said.

"Your father? He's here?"

Dorothy lowered her head and sat quietly with her eyes closed. Caleb took a step forward only to receive a deep growl from Toto that stopped him in his tracks.

"Dorothy?"

She lifted her head, a tear rolled down one cheek. "I'm sorry Caleb. I should've sent word to you sooner. The Southern Marshal tells me how much trouble you've been, trying to find me. In a way, you kept your promise. I have been at my father's side every day since we came over the wall."

He could feel the emotion emanating from Dorothy. Apparently, so could Toto. He stood on all fours and growled loudly. Dorothy sniffed quickly and wiped away the tears as she composed herself

"It's okay Toto, he's a friend. Sit."

Toto obediently sat, but kept a wary eye on Caleb.

Dorothy took a deep breath and expelled it slowly. "I'm sorry I never contacted you. I hadn't seen my father since I was a little girl, and I guess time got away from me."

"It's been months."

"I know."

"It would've taken you a minute to ask someone to…"

She stood up sharply. "I said I was sorry!" Toto was on his feet and growled fiercely. She placed a reassuring hand on Toto to quiet him down. "I see now it was a mistake to ask you to come with me. It was selfish of me to include you in my deal to free my father and me."

"No, Dorothy. I didn't know you found your father. It's just that I've been so worried about you, not knowing whether you were alive or…"

He let his sentence trail off into silence. After a moment, she finished his sentence for him. "Dead?"

"I didn't want to think that. I wouldn't let myself think that."

Neither of them spoke for several minutes, the silence stretching on for what seemed like forever. A thought suddenly occurred to Caleb.

"Are you sure it's your father?"

She gave him a quizzical look. "I think I would know my father."

"Nero made you think he had your father, remember that? But it was just an automaton made to look like him and programmed with your father's memories."

She shook her head. "No. Not this time. It's definitely my father."

"So, you made a deal with the Southern Marshal to be her little errand girl in exchange for our freedom?"

"I'd hoped you, of all people, would understand. My father only has a few years left, and I would like to give him the chance to see the world he missed out on before it's too late."

"Is that worth giving a weapon of indescribable power to the Southern Marshal?"

"I would pay any price to get my father out of this hellhole. It's why I came in the first place. And not you, or anybody, is going to keep me from doing what I came here to do."

Toto picked up on her intensity and began growling. This time he bared some teeth to reflect his utter dislike for Caleb. She stroked his head and he relaxed slightly.

"They promised me they would destroy it as soon as they stopped the threat to OZ."

"Don't you see? There will always be another threat. Another reason to keep a weapon like that around. The people with power always want more power. And now, Nero and the Southern Marshal are the two most powerful people in OZ, and they have joined forces. If you give them that weapon, they will use it to get more power."

A new female voice echoed from the hallway that Nero had disappeared down earlier. "I'm going to stop you there."

The Southern Marshal strode into the room.

"Whatever you think of me, I am more than satisfied to stay here in the Southern Territories. I have no designs on the rest of OZ, or the world for that matter. Nero informs me that should the Brahmastra fall into the Directors' hands, the entire world, even OZ, will fall under their tyranny.

"Now, while I really don't care much about the plight of humans, or the rest of the world for that matter, I do care about the little paradise I have carved out here in the

Southern Territories. And anything that threatens that, must be dealt with, and dealt with swiftly. Nero and I both agree that this weapon is too powerful for anyone to have. We were able to set aside our differences and work together against this common threat to OZ. I had hoped that you would be able to do the same."

Caleb looked from the Southern Marshal to Dorothy. They were both patiently waiting for his answer. He had no idea what to say. On the surface, her argument was sound. But he'd watched how power corrupted even the incorruptible.

The Southern Marshal and Dorothy exchanged a look before the Southern Marshal let out a sigh. "Let me give you some time to think about it. In the meantime, Dorothy and I have some final preparations before she leaves for the northern coast. There are only two exits to this room. If you choose to leave, my offer still stands to take you safely out of the Southern Territories. All you have to do is go out the way you came. There will be an airship waiting for you on the other side of the carriage tube. If you decide to help us, you can join us at the other end of that hallway."

As the Southern Marshal swept out of the room, Dorothy walked up to Caleb, Toto staying glued to her side.

"I do hope you'll change your mind."

She kissed him on the cheek which elicited a subsonic growl from Toto. As they left the room, Toto glanced over his shoulder and bared his teeth with a final snarl. Caleb wasn't sure if Toto's dislike for him was an extension of how Dorothy really felt, or if it was a cat-dog thing.

They disappeared down the hallway, leaving Caleb at the center of the stark white room; alone with his thoughts.

His head swam from the deluge of new knowledge he had gained. Within the past twelve hours, he went from thinking he would never find Dorothy to the discovery that, not only was she alive, but she was working for the person who held her, and her father, prisoner.

He also didn't know if he believed Nero's claim that there was a threat to OZ. But Dorothy believed it. And apparently, the Southern Marshal believed it.

Was there even a threat to OZ? Or was Nero using his proven skills of deception to get his hands on the ultimate weapon? Caleb had been with Nero for his entire life and knew him as well as he knew himself.

But was he the same man who had raised Caleb to be a cold-blooded assassin, or had the fire changed more than Nero's skin, and he really was doing everything in his power to protect OZ? The man he had met in the underground warehouse hours before did not remind him of the man who had trained him to kill, as a child.

He looked from the door that led out to the electrified room and back to the hallway where everyone else had gone down. He, literally, was at a juncture with only two options. Should he press forward and see where life takes him with Dorothy? Or should he turn his back on everything, and everyone, he ever cared about?

The road ahead was guaranteed to be fraught with peril. But would the road back be any less dangerous?

One thing was certain, the road back did not include Dorothy. Whether or not this threat was real, or a play by Nero or the Southern Marshal to get their hands on a powerful weapon, Caleb could not turn his back on Dorothy. He had spent too much of his life playing both sides of the fence. He had done it so effortlessly, it was to the point that people rarely knew what side he was on.

No longer!

If this threat was real, everyone needed his full support; without question.

Filled with a new sense of purpose, and pride, Caleb raced down the hallway to catch up with Dorothy.

The hallway took multiple turns and was longer than Caleb had anticipated. He had been walking for several minutes without seeing a single door or intersecting hallway. He thought maybe he had missed something and decided to turn around after the next corner and go back to see if there were any secret entrances in the walls closer to where he started. He rounded the corner and the hallway terminated at a door up ahead.

Finally.

He jogged up to the door and opened it a crack to peek into the room beyond. The room was empty, so he opened the door all the way and stepped inside.

It wasn't a very large room, probably only about twenty feet by twenty feet with the ceiling rising just above his head. At the other end of the room was a tunnel entrance similar to the one he and Nero had used to come here. But this time there was no carriage.

He stepped on the platform and looked down the tunnel. It was pitch black after only a few feet.

As he stared down into the inky black hole, the edges of his fur started to waft with a light breeze coming from inside the tunnel.

The light breeze quickly became a torrent of air that rushed at him from the tunnel. He took a step back just as a carriage popped out of the hole and stopped on the platform.

The carriage was empty, but he knew they had sent it back for him.

He climbed in the carriage and settled in to the red velvet seat, with his head resting comfortably against the back. He pushed the single button on the control panel and braced himself for the wild ride.

The carriage slowly rolled forward toward the tunnel opening and, as soon as the front of the carriage passed the rim of the tunnel, it shot forward and pressed him into his seat.

This time, there were fewer twists and turns, and the ride was less nerve-racking than the one Nero had taken him on earlier. He peered forward through the front window of the carriage and could see the faint outline of the tunnel stretching straight ahead and terminating in a flickering orange glow.

As the carriage shot forward, the flickering orange glow resolved into roaring flames.

The platform at the other end of this line was on fire.

The carriage blasted through the flames and exited the tunnel. He wasn't going slow enough to stop at the platform. Instead, he was going to collide with the wall on the other side.

Caleb curled into a ball and braced for impact.

The carriage slammed into the opposite wall, glass breaking and metal twisting under the force of the impact. Caleb was thrown to the front of the carriage, but fortunately, if you could still call it fortunate, he crashed into the overstuffed velvet bench seat on the other side. He was stunned, but otherwise unharmed. One of the benefits of having animal DNA was the ability to withstand a greater beating before being broken.

An explosion boomed near the platform and brought Caleb back to reality. He extricated himself from the twisted wreckage and limped onto the platform. Another explosion, this one much closer, knocked him off his feet.

Hands grabbed him and pulled him across the floor to behind a piece of fallen ceiling as bullets chipped off fragments of stone all around the room. The Southern Marshal yelled something in his face, but he could barely hear her over the ringing in his ears. She shoved a repeating carbine rifle into his hands and pointed it in the direction of the door that led out of the carriage platform room. He didn't need to hear what she had said, his eyes told him everything he needed to know. Everything except who was shooting back.

He shook his head to reset his equilibrium and spotted a gun barrel poking its way into the room through the door. He aimed his carbine and fired off a round, driving back the gun barrel.

His hearing slowly returned as he looked around the room. Several of the Southern Marshal's soldiers lay strewn about the room, dead or dying. The Southern Marshal popped up from behind the chunk of ceiling and fired another shot at the door.

She ducked back down and chambered her next round.

Caleb grabbed her shoulder. "What happened?"

"The men sent to replace Nero managed to break out of my jail and secure weapons."

"What about Dorothy?"

"She was back in my castle before any of this started. I'm sure she's fine."

A new sound echoed from beyond the doorway. It sounded like thirty men all firing their carbines in rapid succession. The Southern Marshal laughed and pumped her fist in the air. "Yes!"

Armed soldiers streamed in through the doorway and the Southern Marshal shot at them as they ran in. She ducked as they returned fire but then the same rapid fire that drove the soldiers into the room in the first place echoed again from just outside the door and they all fell down; dead.

The Southern Marshal stood up, a massive grin on her face. She reached down and helped Caleb stand up. "This was not the form of introduction I had expected, but what better way to show you who will be joining you and Dorothy on your quest than a demonstration of what he can do against real opponents?"

Caleb followed her gaze to the door where a large automaton stood, smoke still curling out of the front of the machine gun mounted on the underside of one of his arms.

The Southern Marshal's face beamed with pride. "Caleb, I'd like to introduce you to the only working prototype from the Tin Man project."

She glanced around at the enemy soldiers who had been cut down most expeditiously. "I can see already he will be a welcome addition to your team."

Caleb gawked at the massive automaton. It looked more like an atmospheric diving suit, with every joint a big round ball that made it look like it was built to take abuse and keep on going. The ball jointed arms terminated in large metallic three clawed hands. As menacing as they were, it paled in comparison to the machine gun mounted underneath the right arm. He'd already seen the destructive force of this automated machine gun.

Who, in their right mind, would mount something like that on an independently operating machine?

Maybe humans deserved all the problems they brought down on themselves?

Chapter 5

Caleb flinched as the medic plucked a piece of twisted brass from the wound in his forearm, taking some fur with it. The medic looked over his monocle at Caleb. "If you let me shave it, this would go a lot easier."

"Just do your best."

"The fur's all matted…" He gripped another piece of shrapnel with his pliers and Caleb grimaced through the pain. The medic dropped this new piece on the metal tray to join the others he had already fished out of Caleb's skin. Bits of fur and blood clung to the jagged metal.

"Don't come crying to me when it becomes infected."

"I'll take my chances."

The Southern Marshal stood nearby, conferring with one of her guards. She nodded from what he just told her and approached Caleb. She cleared her throat and startled the medic. He bandaged Caleb's arm quickly and excused himself. She waited until the medic was out of earshot, but still spoke quietly.

"It seems we have seriously underestimated the Directors' true power. My General informs me that, while we have eliminated several small squads of soldiers like the ones in this room, they were all calculated diversions to spread my security forces too thin to prevent the majority of the enemy force from achieving their true objective. Based on the number dead here, and in the other locations, they succeeded in escaping with seventy-five soldiers in their airship."

Caleb reflected on the news that meant he would have some competition in obtaining the weapon. But what stuck out most in his mind was the first thing she had said.

"What do you mean by the Directors' true power?"

"Despite what people on the outside might think, the Southern Territories is a relatively peaceful place. My jail cells were not designed for a large number of prisoners at the same time. I had to divide the captured soldiers among the two cells. That still put about fifty men in each cell designed to hold no more than twenty.

"There are fifteen of their soldiers dead in the jail cell area. They were the ones up against the bars while all fifty men, literally, pushed as one until the doors gave way. The rest, those that we killed in staged battles throughout the castle, also knew they were going to die. They were the distraction while the remainder, the majority, escaped. And that's not the bad news."

"There's bad news?"

"They took Nero."

Caleb's heart sunk.

The Southern Marshal continued. "Nero is the only one who can lead them to the weapon. But he and I already talked about this possible situation. He promised to do his best to delay them, giving us a chance to get to it first. But it gets worse."

Caleb couldn't believe his ears. How could it get any worse than what she had already told him? She didn't leave him wondering as she answered his unspoken question right away.

"Nero still has the key to the box with him. Fortunately, that is only half of the puzzle. They don't know about Dorothy, or that the key won't work without her."

There was a silver lining to this dark cloud after all. Despite everything, Caleb felt the release of tension wash over him. "We don't have to go after the box. It doesn't matter if they get it or not, they still can't open it."

The Southern Marshal shook her head. "They still have an army ten thousand strong coming to OZ in a few days. Nero admitted to me that if he were captured, he could only hold out for so long. Eventually, he will tell them the secret of the key. And then that army will come looking for Dorothy. Without the means to stop them, they will get her, and probably kill all of us in the process."

A new sense of dread completely eradicated the relief he had felt moments before. The Southern Marshal could read the hopelessness in his eyes.

"Don't think like that, Caleb. We still have a chance."

"How can you say that?"

"Because I have the most powerful weapon of all. Knowledge. Follow me."

She led him through the castle to a steel door at the end of a long hallway. Both walls of the hallway were lined with armed guards for its entire length. She paused with her hand on the door latch.

"What I'm about to show you is known only by the people behind this door. Even the guards out here do not know what it is they protect."

As she engaged the latch, he noticed the guards turn away so as not to accidentally catch a glimpse behind the door. Forget about the kind of power the Directors held over their soldiers. He was witnessing the kind of power the Southern Marshal held over hers.

She pushed him ahead of her through the threshold and closed the door behind them. They were in a tiny room, no bigger than a closet, with another door on the other side. There was a steady, rhythmic hum coming from behind the closed door, it sounded like a swarm of bees inside a hive.

She swept past him and opened the door, the low hum rising in pitch as she opened it all the way. Through the open door he saw rows of long tables with people sitting all along the edges staring into boxes that sat on the table in front of them. There must've been over a hundred people in this massive room, each staring into their own illuminated box.

"Two hundred and thirty-five, to be exact."

He snapped out of his reverie and looked at her. "Huh?"

"I have two hundred and thirty-five people here keeping an eye on OZ."

She stepped into the room, lifting her arms to the ceiling and taking in the whole room with her gesture. "Welcome to the Eye of Horus."

"The eye of what?"

"Horus. I named it after an Egyptian goddess whose job it was to watch over and protect her people. Since this room was designed to keep an eye on the hybrids until I could call them home, I felt it was the best name for it."

He looked at one of the boxes. On the face of the box was a small window. The window was illuminated from inside the box and showed people walking back and forth on some crowded street. He had never seen anything like it.

The Southern Marshal beamed with pride. "What you're watching is happening right now on a street in the Western Territories."

He stared at the image in the tiny window. This was not possible. Even if they used thousands of adjustable mirrors and telescopic lenses, there was no way this box could show what was happening hundreds of kilometers away with such definition and clarity. That left only one option. Dark magic. He wasn't one to be taken in by mysticism and the supernatural, but this room was about to make a believer out of him.

The Southern Marshal was at his side. "I know what you're thinking, but you're not even close as to how these work. Professor Gale is a wizard when it comes to the mechanical and electrical sciences. He has drawn up plans for hundreds of amazing things never before seen in all of human, or even hybrid, history. We haven't begun to develop a tenth of what he has already designed. But I must say, out of all the inventions we have attempted to build, this room is part of one of his most impressive systems to date."

"What does it do?"

"Rather than tell you, why don't I show you?"

She whistled, and a small black terrier dog came bounding into the room. It ignored Caleb and stopped right in front of the Southern Marshal, its tail wagging excitedly. She bent down, parted the fur along the back of his neck, and inspected the exposed section of skin. "Jack, switch your display to Toto 819-7532."

"Yes ma'am," Jack replied as he flipped several switches in front of him.

Caleb's jaw dropped as the window showed himself standing in this very room. But it was not like when he looked in a mirror. The view on the window was of him, but from a different angle. He pointed a finger in the air and watched himself in the window as he slowly moved his hand around. He stopped his hand when he noticed he was pointing at himself from the window. He looked to where his hand was pointing, and his hair rose up along his back as he realized he was pointing right at the dog.

She smiled and placed the dog back on the floor. "Go on now. Shoo."

The tiny dog skittered off and Caleb watched as the window on the table showed the room from the dog's perspective as he ran out.

"Professor Gale called them tactical observers. Fully electric automatons that transmit everything they see back to these monitors. It was my idea to build them to look like household pets so they could blend in unnoticed all around OZ.

"Some of them were so indistinguishable from the real thing, using the name tactical observer just seemed so impersonal. The original builders start calling them Totos, and the name stuck."

An unnerving thought suddenly struck Caleb.

"Did you get one of these into the casino?"

"You tell me?"

He thought back to a dog in particular who showed up one day when he was young. When he wasn't looking directly at it, he always got the sense that it was watching him. He hadn't really given it much thought at the time, but that dog outlived all the rest.

He glared at the Southern Marshal, the edge of his lip curling up in anger. "You spied on us? You spied on the hybrids?"

"Only to keep you safe until I could bring you home."

"You snuck into our homes. Into our lives. You violated our privacy."

"I was watching over you."

"That makes it okay?!"

"Of course it was okay. I'm a hybrid, just like you."

"You're not like us!"

"Said the assassin who killed because his human master told him too."

Caleb snapped his mouth shut and his temper boiled just below the surface. The Southern Marshal took a deep breath.

"I fear our conversation is getting off track. I did not show you this room to make you upset. I showed you so, when you leave here to collect the Brahmastra, you know you will not be alone. Even though I will not be with you physically, I will still be watching over you. I will keep you safe. I will keep Dorothy safe. And when the threat is over, I will keep my promise."

He looked deep into her eyes and saw nothing but sincerity. His temper cooled to a low simmer. He didn't dare let it dissipate completely or he might let his guard down. And if growing up in the hardest place in the world had taught him anything, it was to never let your guard down.

She turned back to the monitor station. "Show me Alpha Watch."

"Yes ma'am."

The monitor window shifted to show a dog's point of view of a crowded marketplace. At the center of the view was a boy talking to a shop owner. When the boy finished talking to the owner, he moved on through the crowd and the dog followed him.

There was something very familiar about the boy, but so far Caleb had only seen the back of him. The boy pushed through the crowd without looking around, or glancing behind him. He acted as if he wasn't worried about being followed, or most likely had no idea he was being followed. He stopped occasionally to talk with various shop owners as he made his way through the street market.

She tapped on the glass, indicating the boy. "Nero told us this is the boy who took the Brahmastra. I've had a Toto on him ever since we located him. We haven't seen him with anything remotely like the large chest Nero described, but he's pretty sure the boy knows where it is."

The boy turned around and Caleb's jaw slackened in recognition. He knew this kid, and his name escaped his lips before he could bite his tongue.

"Jasper."

She tilted her head. "You know him?"

"More than I'd like to."

"This will be even easier since you know him. Does he trust you?"

"To be honest, the last time we worked together, he had a hard time figuring out which side I was on. But in the end… Yes, I think he trusts me."

"Excellent. We actually have the edge. Even though they took Nero, and given time, he will lead them to the boy, we don't have to waste precious time looking for the proverbial needle in a haystack. We know exactly where the boy is right now. And we will know exactly where he is when you get there."

"But they have a head start and will get there sooner. What if they find Jasper before we do?"

She indicated the hallway the little dog had run down.

"If you follow me, I can show you why that won't matter."

He let her lead him into another room where the Tin Man and Toto both stood against one wall. The Southern Marshall stopped in front of them.

"You've already seen what the Tin Man and Toto can do. Now let me show you what you can do."

She opened a wardrobe and pointed to several pieces of an armored suit that hung from hooks inside the wardrobe.

"Another one of the Professor's marvelous inventions. We currently have the two prototypes, but we should be able to iron out the final kinks and start ramping up for mass production within a year."

Caleb stared at the two suits of armor in the wardrobe. Rather than being complete suits of armor, they were in individual pieces, designed to be strapped on to various parts of the body separately. A direct hit on the armor might provide some protection, but every joint would still be exposed. And he certainly didn't like hearing that they might not have worked out all the problems yet.

"Is everything we're using a prototype?"

She smiled reassuringly. "Don't worry. The Professor's designs rarely fail."

She grabbed the chest piece off of its hook and spun it around to show Caleb the back. Excitement gleamed in the corner of her eye as she pointed out the two vents on the bottom of the cylinders mounted to the back of the armor.

"This right here is the most amazing bit on this armor. These are jump assist jets. I don't profess to understand what makes them work, but these will help you jump a good eighty to a hundred meters in a single bound. While that's not quite flying, it's pretty damn close."

"Cats were not meant to fly."

She pointed to a unit mounted between the two jets.

"This internal gyrostabilizer here guarantees you will always land on your feet."

He was about to say something he probably would've regretted when a door opened and one of the guards interrupted them.

"Excuse me, ma'am, but you asked me to inform you when she was ready."

The Southern Marshal pushed the armor into Caleb's hands while addressing her guard.

"Excellent. I will be right there."

The guard bowed low and closed the door as he left. Caleb was still staring at the armored jet pack in his hands when the Southern Marshal pointed to the rest of the armor in the wardrobe.

"Put the armor on and be ready to leave in an hour."

She rushed out of the room leaving him standing there, holding what had to be the most terrifying articles of protective clothing known to man, and animal alike. Toto growled quietly as the Tin Man turned to face Caleb. His modulated, metallic voice echoed from a speaker mounted on the front of his chest.

"Don't just stand there, put it on."

Caleb inspected the jet pack in his hands and looked up into the single amber eye of the Tin Man. It was like staring into the eye of some hideous metallic Cyclops, but he wasn't going to let that deter him from pleading his case.

"I don't think you fully understand the risk…"

With a whir of gears, the Tin Man pointed his mounted machine gun directly at Caleb. "Please."

Reluctantly, Caleb donned the suit of armor. It was much lighter, and thinner, than he had expected. It was also a lot more flexible than he thought the armor should be. Even the helmet molded its shape to fit comfortably on his head. The suit covered most of him, but he did not feel protected. It was too light and flexible. He pressed on the chest plate with a finger and the armor depressed enough he could feel the pressure of his finger directly on his chest. What was this? The armor looked impressive from a distance, but this wasn't even going to stop a rock thrown at him by a small child from leaving a bruise. "I'd be better off wearing a thick leather coat than this deceptive piece of pig excrement."

The sound of gears whirring and metal crunching drew his eyes to the Tin Man who had stepped away from the wall, turned to face him, and pointed the large machine gun directly at his chest. He barely had time to raise his hands and protest when the Tin Man shot him.

Chapter 6

The world around him slowed to a snail's crawl as his brain went into overdrive. He had seen what a bullet from this gun could do to a man. The soldiers earlier had been nearly cut in half from the kinetic force unleashed by this terrible weapon. Now, a bullet from that same machine gun had slammed into him at full velocity before he had time to reflect on his past sins.

He was knocked off his feet and skidded across the room on his back until he collided with the far wall. If he hadn't been wearing the helmet, his head would've cracked open upon impact.

He took a sudden breath of air, surprised he wasn't dead. In fact, despite being knocked off his feet and hitting his head on the wall, he hadn't really felt either impact. He must be in shock from the bullet ripping his heart and lungs to shreds. He realized he hadn't felt the bullet pierce his body or his head crack into the wall.

He sat up; and found he could sit up. Not wanting to look, he quickly probed his chest and stomach area with a hand. Instead of feeling a gaping hole where his insides should be spilling out, his hand rubbed against the armor breastplate, and found it was still intact.

He glanced down, letting his eyes confirm that the bullet had not even left a scratch in the armor.

The Tin Man's metallic voice echoed in the room. "Your armor is manufactured from a shear thickening material. The greater the force on the suit, the stronger it becomes. This material provides the maximum protection to the wearer, while still maintaining comfort and flexibility. Another brilliant invention from Professor Gale."

Caleb started to stand up, and was in a half crouch, when the door burst open and guards flooded the room, drawn by the sound of gunfire. Some of them spotted Caleb against the far wall and pointed their rifles at him while shouting commands. He instinctively raised his hands and, at the same time, the Tin Man yelled, "No!"

The jets on his back erupted and he shot up into the air, slamming against the ceiling. Instead of falling back to the ground, the jets kept thrusting and dragged him across the ceiling until he smacked into the wall above the door; and the guards.

The jets cut out and he fell like a stone onto the stunned guards, scattering them in all directions. The guards were back on their feet just as quickly as he was and, in a panic, began firing at him. He was knocked around in what seemed like every direction at once under the barrage of gunfire, his body jerking uncontrollably.

A mechanical voice, amplified louder than the gunfire, shouted, "Cease fire!"

The guards stopped firing and Caleb collapsed forward to his hands and knees. By all rights, he should be dead. He leaned forward on his knees, unharmed, and vomited.

The Tin Man gripped Caleb's arm in a three-fingered claw and lifted him to his feet.

"The suit's jet pack is activated by crouching and raising your arms above your head. I suggest waiting until you're outside to do that again."

Caleb wiped the bile from his lips. "I thought the whatzit rejiggering bopper in the suit was supposed to land me on my feet."

"It's physics, not magic. The room was too small to give the gyrostabilizer time to correct. Like I said, try that again outside and I'm sure you'll have a much better experience."

"What the devil happened in here?"

They turned to see the Southern Marshal gawking at the damage to the room. "I can't leave you two alone for five minutes?"

The Tin Man stepped forward before anybody else could speak. "I was showing Caleb the properties of his new suit. Your guards were assisting me in demonstrating the suit's anti-ballistics effectiveness."

A piece of wall, damaged by the numerous rounds that had pelted it, took that precise moment to collapse to the floor in a cloud of dust. The Southern Marshal shook her head. "Next time, take it outside."

She motioned to Caleb. "Come with me."

The suit stiffened when he tried to run, almost as if it resisted him. The same thing that gave the suit its hardness must also get activated when he moved too quickly. He soon developed a smooth rhythm, and was able to catch up with the Southern Marshal. "What magical gift are you going to bestow upon me next?"

"Nothing. I'm presenting you before the Council of Elders."

"The Council of Elders? Why?"

She continued walking at a fast pace. "Despite what it looks like, I'm not in charge here. I use my status as the Marshal over the Southern Territories to do what the Council tells me."

"They told you to dress me up in this monkey suit and parade me around in front of them?"

She stopped sharply. "No. That was my idea. They told me to pack my things and be ready to run with the rest of the hybrids."

"Run?"

She slammed a balled fist on his chest plate, the suit absorbing the impact so well, he didn't feel the slightest vibration.

"We have a chance, actually have a chance, to change our destiny. And do you know what those idiots want us to do? They want us to run with our tails firmly between our legs. I'm taking you in front of them to prove we don't have to run anymore. This suit, the Tin Man, even Toto, gives us a fighting chance to get the Brahmastra before the humans do. And I say we take that chance."

Her words had an unexpected effect on him. She had finally voiced the plight of the hybrids, and she was right. It was time they took charge of their own destiny and stopped letting the humans push them around, or force them to live behind barriers and walls, just to feel safe.

He stood up straighter and looked the Southern Marshal squarely in the eye. "What do you need from me?"

A smile spread across her lips. "You've just given it. If I can convince you, together we can convince the Council."

He felt good about this new plan of action. Maybe it was time for him to take his rightful place as leader of the hybrids. The Council had done what they could to hide them and protect them. Now that there was a direct threat to their very existence, hiding was no longer an option. And it looked like it was up to him to lead his people through the dawn of a new era.

The Southern Marshal clapped a hand on his shoulder. "Let's go tell those old geezers…"

An explosion echoed in the distance moments before the ground rumbled under their feet. Dust filtered down from the newly formed cracks in the ceiling. The Southern Marshal ran over to a speaker mounted on the wall and pushed down on the button next to it. "Report!"

A voice crackled through the speaker. "The castle is under attack, ma'am."

"Establish a defense perimeter. Nobody gets into the castle. Is that understood?"

"Yes ma'am!"

She released the button on the speaker and gripped Caleb's shoulders with a huge smile on her face. "This couldn't have come at a better time. You get out there, stop whoever's attacking the castle, and prove to the Council of Elders that you are the one."

Caleb tried to swallow, but his mouth had dried up. His silence told the Southern Marshal more than he ever could with words. She patted his shoulder reassuringly.

"It would've been nice to properly train you on how to use the suit, rather than force you to learn it as you go. Don't worry, the Tin Man will help you."

As if on cue, the Tin Man bounded down the hallway, if bounded was the right word for the massive metallic beast that moved swiftly toward them, moving much faster than his squat and bulbous shape should allow.

Explosions continued to bellow and shake the ground under their feet. The Southern Marshal jabbed a thumb over her shoulder. "Get out there before they reduce my castle to rubble."

The Tin Man pointed his machine gun at the far wall and fired a single shot. The wall exploded outward from the solitary round. Caleb gawked at the Tin Man, whose metallic voice echoed in the small hallway.

"I have three types of rounds for my gun. One of them explodes on impact. I'm afraid you only have standard ammunition for your suit gun."

Caleb looked down at his suit. He didn't see any gun mounted on the underside of either arm. The forearm pieces of his suit were a bit bulky along the inside of his arms, but no gun anywhere.

"My suit gun?"

"Make a fist with your right hand and crook your index finger out slightly."

Caleb balled his hand into a fist and then poked his index finger out slightly. A gun barrel snapped out from the armor along the top of his hand and a trigger sprang out to rest against his index finger. The gun was integrated into the suit of armor. He opened his hand and everything receded back into the suit. He rolled his left hand into a fist and a double-edged sword, as long as his forearm, sprang out along the top of his hand. He opened his hand, and it retracted just as quickly.

This suit was more than just defensive protection. It was combat ready.

The Southern Marshal slapped a hand on his back. He heard it rather than felt it.

"You learn quickly, Caleb. Now get out there and show those bastards that the hybrids are no longer going to roll over and take it."

The Tin Man was the first through the hole in the wall. Caleb followed him through the castle wall and out into the blinding sun.

All around him, portions of the castle were on fire, columns of black and gray smoke billowing into the clear blue sky.

The Tin Man was scanning the skies. "I don't see the airship."

Caleb looked up and saw only blue sky and columns of dark smoke.

"It's camouflaged. If we get somewhere high, we can look for the shadow it casts on the ground."

"Excellent idea. Follow me."

The Tin Man half-crouched and raised his arms in the air. Plumes of flame shot out from his back and he vaulted into the air and onto the roof of the nearest building. He used the height of that building to jump again to the roof of the next tallest tower. And then he was out of sight.

The Tin Man made it look so easy. But Caleb remembered what happened inside the room. He had never felt so out of control in his life. The first time hadn't given him a chance to get a feel for the suit, other than the feeling of sheer panic. Now he was expected to repel an attacking force with it?

An explosion directly above blew chunks of stone away from the top of a castle tower. He instinctively ducked while raising his arms to protect his head from the falling debris.

The jets activated on his unintentional command. He shot into the air and his stomach flipped upside down.

To the casual observer, he flew off into the air with a battle cry. But he was actually screaming in terror as the ground fell away.

He flailed his arms and legs, trying to stay upright, but it was not needed. As promised, the suit maintained a steady course as he descended to the rooftop of the nearest building. He settled onto the roof with no more effort than hopping down from the bottom rung of a ladder.

The Tin Man landed on a roof several buildings away and jumped again. Caleb looked in the direction the Tin Man was headed. There it was. The long airship-shaped shadow crawled across the rooftops just ahead of the Tin Man.

A puff of smoke erupted in the middle of the clear blue sky. The Tin Man angled sideways and narrowly avoided the cannonball fired at him. His jets pushed him higher until he crashed into a piece of the sky itself. He clung to the sky with a three-fingered claw and tore away a section with his other claw to reveal the airship.

Now that they had a target, cannons on the ground began firing, and hitting, the airship.

The Tin Man let go and dropped out of sight between two buildings.

Once the airship was targetable, it turned tail and fled out of range of the castle's defenses.

The Tin Man landed on the roof next to him. "Excellent work, Caleb. They will think twice before trying that again"

"I didn't do anything."

"I will be glad to have you join our quest."

Caleb just shook his head.

Caleb stood in the center of a large circular chamber next to the Tin Man and the Southern Marshal. The three of them faced the nine members of the Council of Elders. The Eldest sat at the center with four younger, but not by much, elders seated on either side of him. It was obvious he did not like hearing the words that were coming out of his own mouth.

"The votes have been cast and the Council has decided, on a vote of five to four I might add, to allow your little expedition to retrieve the Brahmastra. Now before you congratulate each other on your little victory here today, let me add that this is the first time the counsel has been divided on an issue of this magnitude. Since the window of time to succeed with such a far-fetched plan is so small, the Council has wisely decided to continue with plans to leave OZ and find a new home; beyond the reach of humans."

The Southern Marshal leaned over and whispered to Caleb. "I bet I can guess which way the Eldest voted."

The Eldest slammed his fist on the table and stood abruptly. "Do not make a mockery of me, or of the Council. The only reason we even voted on your scheme in the first place is because the stakes are so high. And, so help me, it pains me to admit that the future of all hybrids might actually rest squarely on your misguided shoulders.

"Look at yourselves. You, Madam Marshal. You're just barely a hybrid. You could live comfortably among the humans unnoticed and unharmed. I applaud your strength of conviction when it comes to the plight of our people.

"But look who you selected as the heroes of your quest. A leader, who has spent so much time among humans, he refuses to take his place as the leader of our people. And a robot. Need I say more?"

The youngest elder was the first to reply. "No. You don't."

The Eldest turned on him. "Excuse me?"

"You made your statement when you voted. The last thing these brave souls need to hear is that we don't believe in them, because we do."

"Only half of us do."

"No. I believe the vote revealed that more than half did."

The Eldest laugh. "By one vote."

"One vote was all it took. But do not berate those who would come to our defense because that one vote went against how you voted."

The Eldest raised his voice. "You do not know how I voted. They are cast in secret."

"Oh please. Your speech, given in front of the only ones willing to stand up to the humans, told me your vote. And since I was willing to speak out against your tirade, everyone knows how I voted. The rest of the votes can remain a secret." He faced the three standing at the center of the room. "But I want you to know that you have my full support."

The Eldest banged his gavel and stared distastefully at the three of them in the center of the room.

"This special meeting of the Council is adjourned. We will convene again in one week's time. The location depends upon your actions. And, for the record, a house divided cannot stand. While you did not get my vote, you still get my support."

One by one, the rest of the elders in the Council also replied, "And my support."

The Southern Marshal spoke up. "Thank you, all of you. My team will depart immediately and, let me assure you, we will win."

The Eldest's shoulders dropped as he looked sadly at the three of them. "Let's hope, for all our sakes, you are right."

The Southern Marshal spun around and exited the chamber, Caleb and the Tin Man following right behind. As soon as they were outside the council chamber, she spoke quickly.

"We were lucky they decided to attack the castle like they did. It means they gave up their head start. We have an excellent chance of getting there twenty-four hours ahead of them, even if they push their airship to its top speed."

The Tin Man's modulated voice echoed in the long hallway. "I thought their airship was the fastest in the sky. How are we supposed to get there ahead of them?"

The Southern Marshal walked swiftly as she gave her cryptic reply. "The Southern Territories are not as cut off from the rest of OZ as I have led everyone to believe."

She led them through several twists and turns deep under her castle and into a small room where a cylinder carriage waited on the platform at this end of another tunnel.

"The carriage will take you to a city on the other side of the wall that separates the Southern Territories from the rest of OZ."

Caleb looked around at the empty room.

"I thought Dorothy and Toto were coming."

"They have already gone ahead. A friend of Nero's will meet you in the city and take you to them. Now go, quickly. I have cannons on the border that will do their best to slow down the airship, but I doubt we can stop it when we can barely see it. You have to maintain your lead if we have any hope of keeping the weapon out of human hands."

Caleb and the Tin Man settled into the carriage. The Southern Marshal held on to the curved glass door and looked at both of them.

"Good luck."

She lowered the curved glass door and twisted the lock. Her cloak flapped angrily from the sudden wind as the carriage pulled away from the platform and into the darkness of the tunnel.

Chapter 7

The clock was ticking. And not just because of the humans who were racing to get to the weapon first. Even if the Southern Marshal destroyed the airship before it crossed over the wall, there was still the matter of the thousand-airship armada due to land in OZ in less than a week. And they still had to make their way through all of OZ to get to the Northern Territories, find Jasper, and then locate the hidden weapon.

Maybe if OZ had an army equipped with suits like his, or even a hundred more Tin Men, they could repel the invading force.

Instead, it was just the two of them. And he barely knew how to use his own suit.

The carriage rocketed through the pitch black underground tunnel. There was no difference between eyes open or eyes closed. It felt like they'd been traveling through the dark for half the day when a pinpoint of light appeared ahead. They were nearing the other end of the tunnel.

The circle of light expanded until they shot out the other end of the tunnel and quickly skidded to a stop at a platform.

Someone opened the door and several rifle barrels appear in the doorway of the carriage, accompanied by the unmistakable clicks of hammers being cocked.

A burly man, his scalp shaved bald and covered in tattoos, poked his head through the door and smiled a teeth-blackened grin.

"Well, whadaya know. Tell Ellis we got two more of 'em."

Chapter 8

The guns retreated back through the door of the carriage and the bald tattooed man's voice called out to them.

"Come on out. And don't try anything funny. I got twenty guns out here, and every one of them's on a hair trigger."

The Tin Man placed a claw on Caleb's shoulder and spoke softly through the speaker. "I suggest we do as they ask until we can properly assess the situation. No sense showing them their guns cannot harm us until we know what's going on."

Caleb nodded and stepped out of the carriage and onto the platform. He quickly assessed there were at least twenty gun barrels pointed at him. Every one of them held by men with bulging muscles and shaved heads. Every arm, shoulder, neck and head in the room was covered in tattoos. The tattoos disappeared into the clothing, leading him to think they might even cover their entire body. It's silly what people did to themselves when they didn't have fur.

The Tin Man stepped out of the carriage and rose to his full height of nearly eight feet tall. The men all took a half step backward and concentrated their guns on him instead of Caleb.

The only guy without a gun was also the only one who spoke. "Is one of you named Caleb?"

Caleb looked at the large man with tattoos, his voice cracked a little on his first attempt at a reply and he coughed and swallowed twice before saying again, "I am."

"Ellis wants to talk to you. Follow me."

Caleb looked to the Tin Man for guidance. He didn't move, but his speaker crackled softly. "Go see what he wants. I'll be okay here."

None of the men took their guns away from the Tin Man as Caleb walked past them and followed Tattoo Head through the door.

He paused at a door halfway down the hallway. As soon as Caleb reached him, he opened it.

"Ellis is inside. He's been expecting you."

Caleb stepped through the door and Tattoo Head closed it behind him. He heard the faint sound of a lock being engaged. He wasn't getting back through that door until they let him out.

The room was lit by candles that flickered throughout the room while a hotly burning fire popped and crackled in the fireplace, the mantle above it was adorned with various trophies, medals, and ribbons. The sweet smell of cherry wood was at odds with the musty stench of old smoke. His eyes adjusted quickly to the semi-darkness. It looked like a sitting room, or a parlor room, from one of the more opulent houses people built in OZ. Various sofas and lounges were placed symmetrically about the room with two overstuffed chairs canted at an angle in front of the roaring fireplace.

One of the chairs was empty, but the one with its back to him had the telltale curl of smoke rising up above it. Someone was seated in the other chair, and whoever they were had spent a lot of time smoking in this room.

A hand, holding a pipe, poked out from the side of the chair and motioned to the empty chair.

"Please, have a seat Caleb."

Caleb walked cautiously around to the front of the empty chair and sat down. The man was a distinguished looking older gentleman, the polar opposite of the shaved and tattooed ruffians outside. His silver-white hair was combed neatly back and his beard trimmed to perfection. He puffed on his pipe while staring up at the awards on the mantle.

"Why would someone keep reminders of a life that once was, when the life you are living now, is what is most important?"

He shifted in his chair and gave Caleb the once-over with his eyes.

"You're a tad shorter than I was hoping for. Anyone who tells you that size doesn't matter is a fool. When you're going up against the Directorate Army, bigger is always better."

Caleb didn't know what to say, or how to respond to this man who puffed on his pipe and blew out the smoke in a long breath.

"But beggars can't be choosers. We play with the hand we're dealt."

Caleb had expected something more, something profound, from how this man looked, dressed, and acted. Instead, he spat out tired old expressions.

"Are you going to tell me how you knew my name, or are you just going to sit there and regale me with platitudes?"

The man puffed on his pipe. "Why are you doing this?"

The man had not answered him, and instead replied with a question of his own. Caleb decided to play the game a little longer before letting his temper get the better of him.

"Why am I doing what?"

"Why have you embarked on this little quest?"

Somehow, this man knew what he was doing. Time to put that knowledge to the test, or see if this old man was fishing.

"I've been asked to retrieve something of immense value to the history of the hybrid people."

Smoke filtered between the man's teeth as he chuckled. "Immense value. I like how you put that. But it's not just valuable to the hybrids. If it's true what this weapon can do, it's valuable to anybody who gets their hands on it, or paws, as the case may be."

So, the man knew everything. It would make no sense to hide anything from him then.

"So, are you going to help us, or do you have demands of your own."

The man smiled with half his mouth while the other half puffed on his pipe. He exhaled another long stream of smoke and pointed to the mantle with his pipe.

"Every one of those awards was given to me for my service in the Directorate Army. They are a constant reminder of what I gave up the day I realized that what the Directors had planned for the world was not peace.

"We were a small group, working from the inside to stop them. Emboldened by a few meaningful successes in hindering the

Directors' rise to world power, we began to recruit with a little less, shall I say, discretion. Here we were, spies working against the Directors from within their organization. We were so full of ourselves, we hadn't realized, until it was too late, that the Directors had planted a spy of their own.

"When everything came crashing down around us, those too cowardly to kill themselves before being captured, were sent here to live out the rest of their days in exile. By not making our treasonable actions punishable by death, the Directors sent a clear message. Our cause fizzled and died because people are more willing to risk death than they are willing to risk life imprisonment."

He studied Caleb intently.

"But you. You're already in prison. All you have left to wager is your life. Before you put your life on the line, decide what it is you're risking it for. Is it worth it?"

Caleb immediately thought of Dorothy. He had made a vow to himself to help her no matter the cost. He nodded his head.

"It's worth it."

"Are you sure she's worth it?"

Caleb's mouth hung open. How did he know he was doing it for Dorothy? As if reading his mind, the man answered.

"Nero and I do not keep secrets from each other. Fortunately for the cause, the Directors did not catch everyone. So, even after all this time, we still have someone on the inside keeping the Directors from achieving their goal of world conquest. Right now, our first priority is to keep your ancient hybrid weapon out of the Directors' hands.

"If I thought you were doing this to prove yourself worthy as their leader, or to help reinstate the hybrids to the status as gods they enjoyed so long ago, I would have ordered my men to kill you as soon as you arrived.

"But you're doing this for love. Love of a human, no less. I can't think of any cause more worthy than that. I can get you as far north as Center City. After that, you're on your own."

The man stood up and tapped his pipe out into an ashtray.

"Come on, let's get you back with your team and on the road as soon as possible."

Caleb followed him out of the room and back to the transport platform. The Tin

Man, Toto and Dorothy stood to one side. Nobody was pointing their guns at them, or even paying any real attention to them. Caleb rushed into the room and up to Dorothy.

"Dorothy, are you okay?"

She looked at him, confusion written all over her face. "Do I know you?"

He smiled, allowing some of his own confusion to scrawl across his face. "It's me, Caleb."

Her eyes darted back and forth, as if she were desperately trying to recall something important. "Caleb… Caleb… Ah yes! I have a message for you from the Southern Marshal."

She closed her eyes and her face lost all expression. "I promised to give you Dorothy. However, until you have completed your task, I only give you her body to protect. Her memories will be restored when you return with the Brahmastra. Until then, keep your scarecrow safe."

Dorothy's eyes opened and her face returned to the quizzical expression. "Did I just say something?"

Caleb turned on the old man. "What is this?!"

He shrugged his shoulders. "I wouldn't know. That's how she was when she arrived."

That wasn't good enough. He had been tricked, and he wasn't going to stand for it.

"I want to speak with her."

"She's standing right there."

"Not her! The Southern Marshal. I want to speak with her now!"

"Sorry, son. Can't help you there."

"You must communicate with her somehow. She's at the other end of your tunnel."

"It's an asynchronous relationship. She sends food and, on occasion, messages down the line. I have explicit instructions to always send the carriage back empty. She has made it clear that if I ever break our agreement, she will seal the tunnel, and our fate."

What was he talking about? If memory served him correctly, this city was surrounded by vast farmlands that fed most of the Western Territories. Why did he have to rely on food from the Southern Marshal?

"How is your fate tied to her?"

"OZ is not the same place you left six months ago. Say what you will about the Eastern and Western Marshals. Their heavy-handed rule kept the people in line. With them gone, lawlessness has become the order of the day. My city has been under siege for nearly two months now. If it were not for the Southern Marshal, we would have starved to death a month ago. Her continued assistance is dependent upon my getting you past that siege and on your way. And that is what I intend to do."

Caleb looked at the scarecrow who used to be Dorothy. His Dorothy.

He decided he would get the Brahmastra and use it to force the Southern Marshal to return Dorothy's memories. Then he would take her, and her father, out of OZ forever.

The Adventure Continues...

Other Books by the Author

A is for Apprentice (Fantasy)

Oliver Twist: Victorian Vampire (Fantasy)

A Tale of Two Cities with Dragons (Fantasy)

Shade Infinity (Science Fiction Thriller)

Peacekeepers X-Alpha Series (Thriller)
>   Inherit the Throne
>   The Warrior's Code

Steampunk OZ Series (Science Fiction Serial)
>   Forgotten Girl
>   The Legacy's World

Emerald Shadow

The Future's Destiny

The Dangerous Captive

Missing Legacy

Shadow of History

The Edge of the Hunter

Fugue: The Cure (Science Fiction Short Story)

Stay informed about all the trouble I keep getting into. Subscribe to Steve DeWinter's Book Report (i.e. the mailing list) @ SteveDW.com